This magical book belongs to:

....

Buttercup's Pod

Fairy Godmother's Palace

Cinema

Ice Cream Parlour

Fairy School of Magic & Music

Tabitha's Pod

SPARKLE TREE FOREST

To all the children in the world who
believe in fairies and magic. K.H.

To Hilary, who shakes the fairy dust. S.W.

HODDER CHILDREN'S BOOKS

First published in Great Britain in 2014 by Hodder Children's Books
This edition published in 2017 by Hodder and Stoughton

3 5 7 9 10 8 6 4 2

Text copyright © Katharine Holabird, 2014
Illustrations copyright © Sarah Warburton, 2014

The moral rights of the author and illustrator have been asserted.

A CIP catalogue record for this book
is available from the British Library.

ISBN 978 1 444 93950 7

Printed in China

Hodder Children's Books
An imprint of
Hachette Children's Group
Carmelite House 50 Victoria Embankment London EC4Y 0DZ
An Hachette UK Company
www.hachette.co.uk

Twinkle

Katharine Holabird and Sarah Warburton

Hodder Children's Books

A division of Hachette Children's Books

Twinkle's wings were
glowing with excitement!

"Tra-la-la-la-la!" she sang.
"I'm a little fairy
with sparkling wings.
When I get my magic wand,
I'll do amazing things!"

It was Twinkle's first day at
The Fairy School of Magic and Music
and she couldn't wait to learn fancy
spells like all the big fairies.

Twinkle skipped in line with all the little fairies waiting for wands.
Her wish came true when she got a sparkling peachy pink one!
Shiny fairy notebooks and glittery pens appeared on all the desks.

Welcome to Fairy School

Buttercup
Izzybell   Pippa
Lulu   Tabitha
Petal   Twinkle

"We'll start with a simple spell," said Miss Flutterbee.

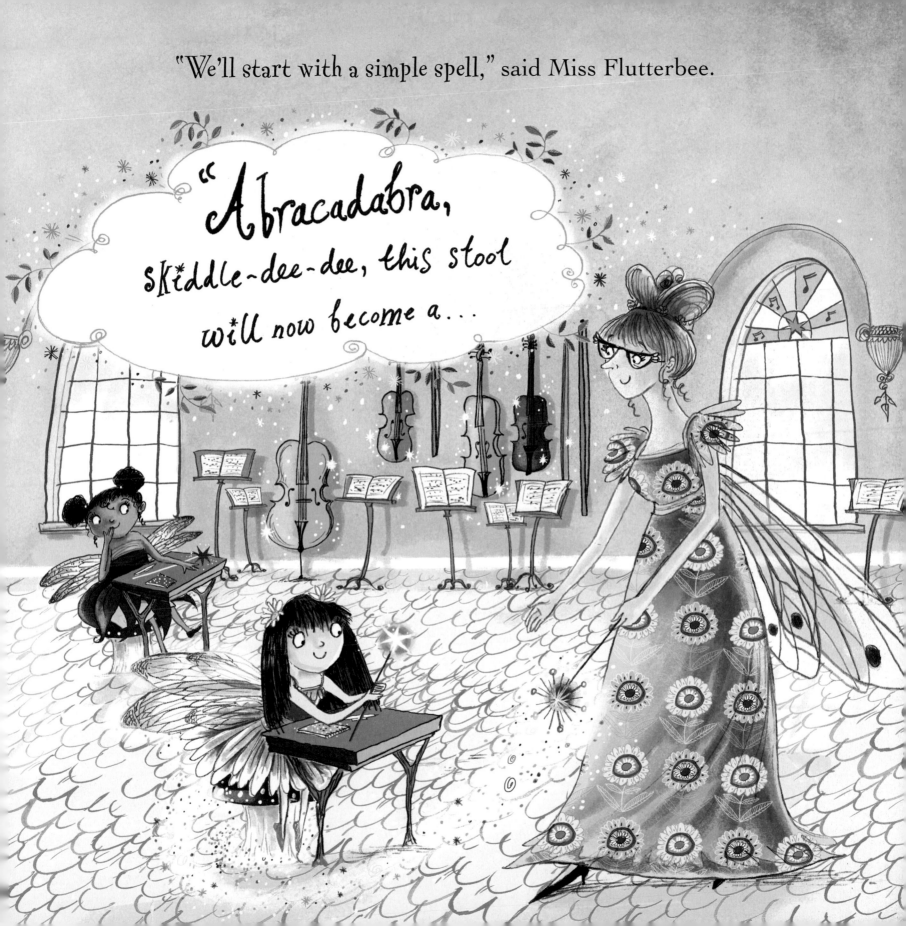

"Abracadabra, skiddle-dee-dee, this stool will now become a..."

...tree!"

Before she could blink, Twinkle found herself perched way
up in a pear tree with Pippa and Lulu waving below.

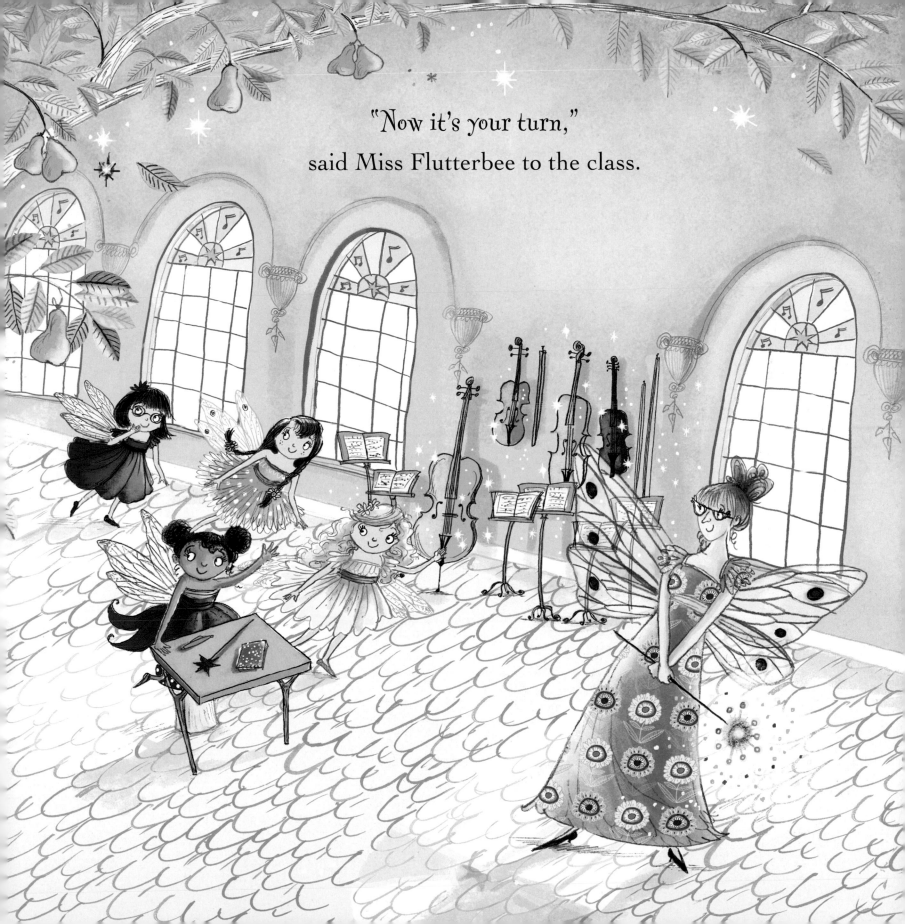

"Now it's your turn,"
said Miss Flutterbee to the class.

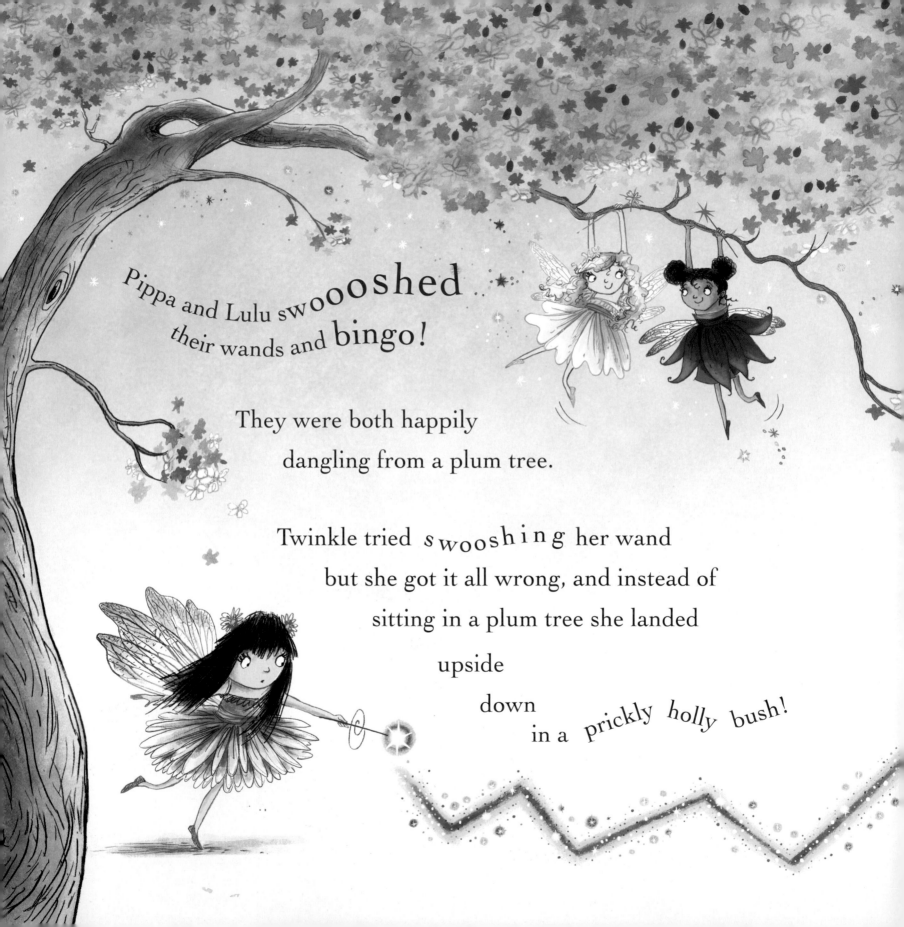

Pippa and Lulu swooooshed their wands and bingo!

They were both happily dangling from a plum tree.

Twinkle tried swooshing her wand but she got it all wrong, and instead of sitting in a plum tree she landed upside down in a prickly holly bush!

"Ouch!" cried Twinkle,
and Miss Flutterbee had to rescue her.

"Now remember to practise at home," said
Miss Flutterbee. "But **no** spells at night
– you don't want to start a ruckus."

That afternoon, Twinkle and her friends did their homework together.

"This is fun!" said Pippa, turning a teapot into a tiara.

"I love doing spells," said Lulu, changing bananas into balloons.

But Twinkle's swooshes were rather clumsy, and so her spells just got sillier and **sillier.**

"Don't worry, Twinks," said Pippa and Lulu, "we can practise again tomorrow."

That night,
Twinkle was in such
a tizzy she couldn't
sleep a wink, and she
forgot all about
Miss Flutterbee's
warning.

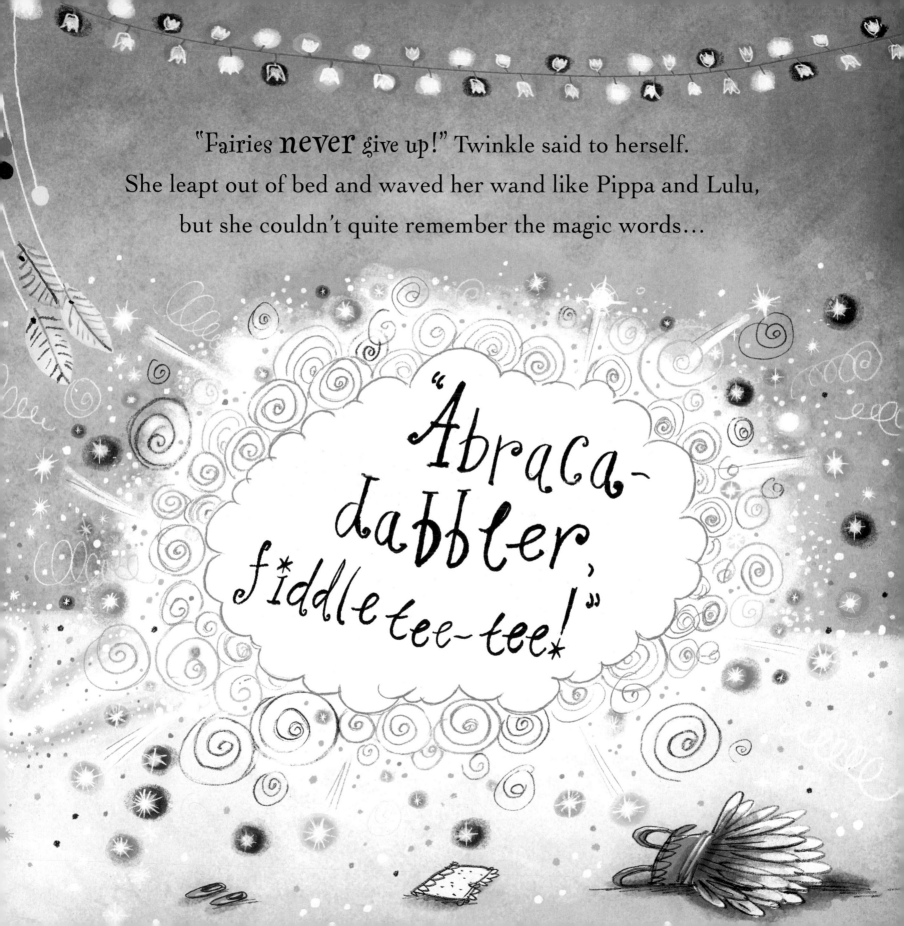

"Fairies **never** give up!" Twinkle said to herself.
She leapt out of bed and waved her wand like Pippa and Lulu,
but she couldn't quite remember the magic words...

"Abraca-dabbler, fiddle tee-tee!"

Her wings fluttered wildly
as the bed began swinging,

the rocking chair
started rocking,

the alarm clock kept ringing,
and the lights were flashing.

Twinkle's cosy little fairy pod was shaking
and swaying, banging and clanging.

"HELP!" shouted Twinkle as the rumpus continued.

One by one all the creatures in Sparkle Tree Forest woke up, and they were not very happy… Bumble bees and ladybirds buzzed, grumpy gremlins and bullfrogs croaked, and groggy birds and bats fell out of the trees.

"Whooooooo's making that racket?" screeched the owl.

"Stop the ruckus!" shouted the squirrel.

"Fiddlesticks and fairy cakes!" said Twinkle, waving her wand faster and faster, but the crashing and banging only got louder.

The next morning, every creature in the forest was howling and complaining outside Twinkle's door.

"Sorry about my silly spells," said Twinkle,
and she dashed off to see Miss Flutterbee.

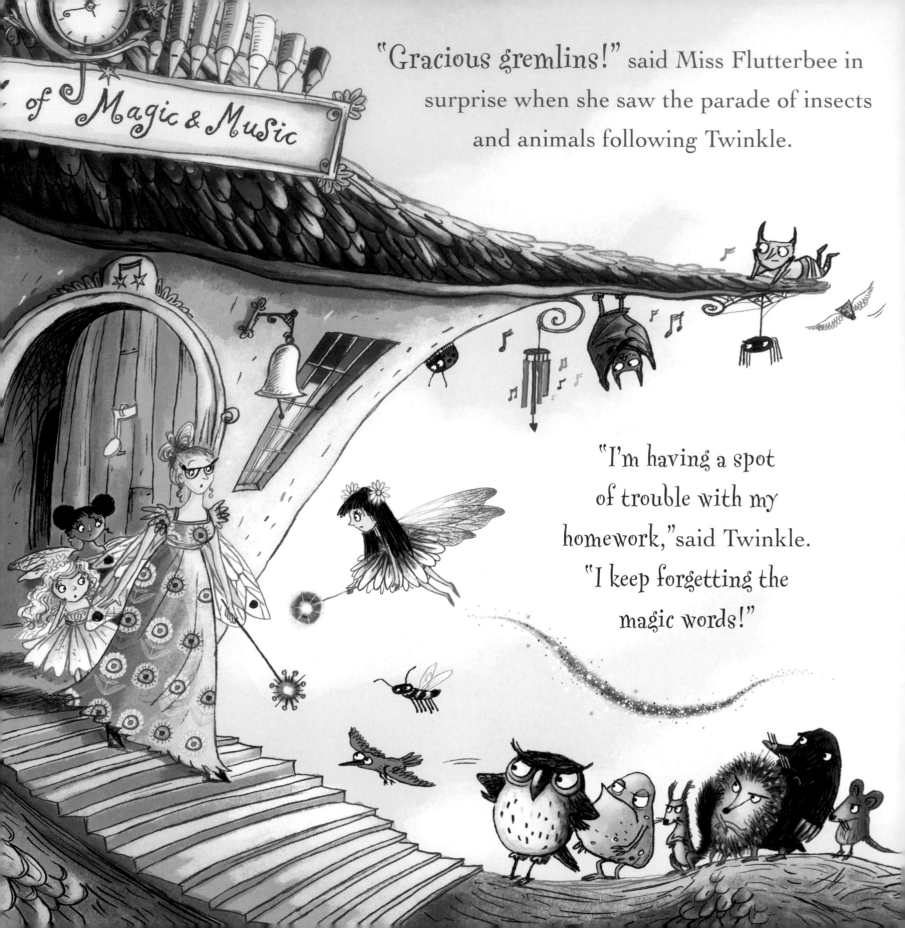

of **Magic & Music**

"Gracious gremlins!" said Miss Flutterbee in surprise when she saw the parade of insects and animals following Twinkle.

"I'm having a spot of trouble with my homework," said Twinkle. "I keep forgetting the magic words!"

"Since you love to sing, try **singing** your spells instead. Maybe that will help you remember," suggested Miss Flutterbee kindly.

"Brilliant!" said Twinkle, and her wings glowed bright pink again.

After school that day, Twinkle flew home singing the magic words.

"Abracadabra, skidddle-dee-dee, fix the mess that's up in my tree."

And when she arrived, Twinkle was overjoyed to see everything was back in its place again.

As the sun set over Sparkle Tree Forest, Twinkle sprinkled fairy dust over the treetops and sang a lullaby to all the forest creatures, just to make sure they all had a really good sleep.

"Good night, sleep tight, with sweet dreams in your head.

Tomorrow we'll have lots of fun, but now it's time for bed!"

Lulu's Pod

Twinkle's Pod

Izzybell's Pod

Petal's Pod

Pippa's Pod

Gallery

Wand shop

Miss Flutterbee's Pod

Café

Dress Shops

Library

Buttercup's Pod

Fairy Godmother's Palace

Fairy School of Magic & Music

Tabitha's Pod

Cinema

Ice Cream Parlour

SPARKLE TREE FOREST

Enjoy more sparkling
Tw*nkle stories

By the author of
Angelina Ballerina

Tw*nkle

Katharine Holabird and Sarah Warburton

By the author of
Angelina Ballerina

Tw*nkle
Thinks Pink!

Katharine Holabird and Sarah Warburton